THE GHOST-EYE TREE

By Bill Martin, Jr. and John Archambault

Illustrated by
Ted Rand

SQUARE FISH

Henry Holt and Company/New York

One dark and windy autumn night
when the sun had long gone down,
Mama asked my sister and me
to take the road
to the end of the town
to get a bucket of milk.

Oooo . . .
I dreaded to go . . .
I dreaded the tree. . . .
Why does Mama always choose me
when the night is so dark
and the mind runs free?

"Come on, 'fraidy cat!"
 my sister said.
"Don't hang back!"

"I'm not hangin' back,"
 I said.
"I'm getting my hat."

"Your dumb hat,"
 my sister said.
"It's too big for you.
 It makes you look stupid."

"Well, you don't have to wear it,"
 I said.

"No, but I have to look at it,"
 my sister said.

"Then look the other way,"
 I said.

Oooo . . .
how dark it was . . .
how dread it was . . .
walking the road
to the end of the town . . .
for the halfway tree . . .
the Ghost-Eye tree . . .
was feared by all . . .
the great and the small . . .
who walked the road
to the end of the town. . . .

"What's the matter now?"
  my sister said.

"My hat,"
  I said.
"It slipped off."

"You're afraid, that's what!"
  my sister said.

"I am not,"
  I said.
"I'm getting my hat."

As we neared the tree,
our walk slowed down . . .
halfway down
to the end of the town . . .
hiding what we feared the most . . .
pretending there would be no ghost . . .
pretending . . .
not to be . . .
afraid. . . .

"There's nothing to fear,"
my sister said.
"There's nothing here
but an old oak tree."

"No, there's nothing here,"
I said.
"There's nothing to fear
in an old oak tree."

But we ran past the tree
as fast as we could. . . .
Nothing happened!
Nothing happened!
We felt so good
that we started to sing,
"There's no such thing
as a ghost!
There's no such thing
as a ghost!"

"It's only a dream,"
my sister said.
"It's only a fooly
inside your head.
There's nothing to dread
in an old oak tree."

I pulled my hat down
over one eye . . .
to look tough
like Mike Barber
in the movies.
I'm tough!
I said to myself.
Real tough!

"What?"
my sister said.

"I didn't say anything,"
I said.

"You did too!"
my sister said.
"You were muttering to yourself."

"I was not,"
I said.

"Then push up your hat,"
my sister said,
"You look stupid."

Oh,
how glad were we,
how free to be
walking the road
to the end of the town . . .
for the halfway tree,
the Ghost-Eye tree,
my sister and I
had passed it by . . .
and the road led down
to the end of the town
where we got the bucket of milk.

"That's a fine hat you got,"
  said Mr. Cowlander, the milkman.

I smiled.

" 'Twould make a good milk bucket,"
  said Mr. Cowlander.

My sister laughed.
I didn't.

Nobody's gonna put milk in my hat,
  I said to myself.

"What?"
  said Mr. Cowlander.

"I didn't say anything,"
  I said.

"Yes, you did,"
  my sister said.
"You were muttering again.
  Mr. Cowlander,
  that hat makes him crazy.
  It's a crazy hat!"

"Well, come on,"
  I said.
"Help me carry the milk."

First, I carried . . .
then my sister carried . . .
walking home
from the end of the town . . .
we couldn't walk fast,
the milk slowed us down . . .
walking home
from the end of the town. . . .

Oooo, how dark . . .
Oooo, how dread. . . .

"Hurry up,"
 my sister said.
"We're halfway home."

"Oooo, what's that?"
 I said.

"I didn't hear anything."
 my sister said.

"But I heard . . . something . . ."
 I said.
"I really heard it . . .
 Let's go back to Mr. Cowlander's."

"No . . . no!"
 my sister said.
"There's nothing here,
 nothing to fear. . . ."

Oooo . . .
why does Mama always choose me
when the night is so dark
and the mind runs free. . . .

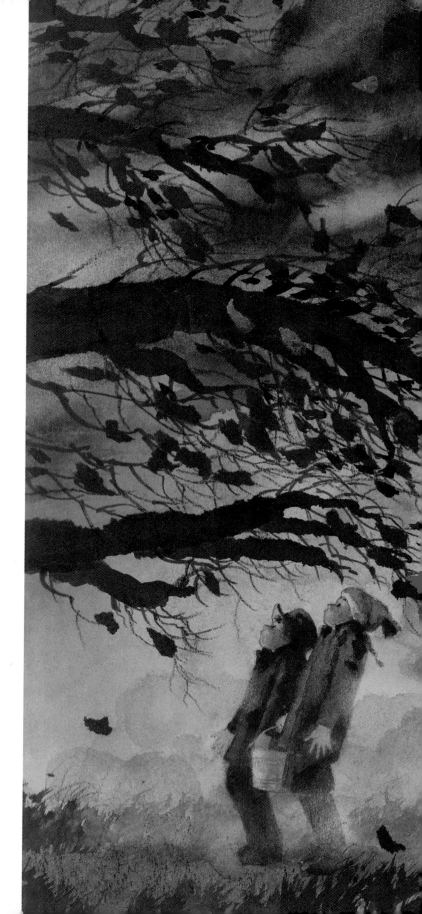

Oooo . . .
look . . . look . . .

The halfway tree,
the Ghost-Eye tree . . .
turned its head
and looked at me. . . .

Oooo . . .

The halfway tree . . .
the Ghost-Eye tree . . .
shook its arms . . .
and reached . . .
for ME!

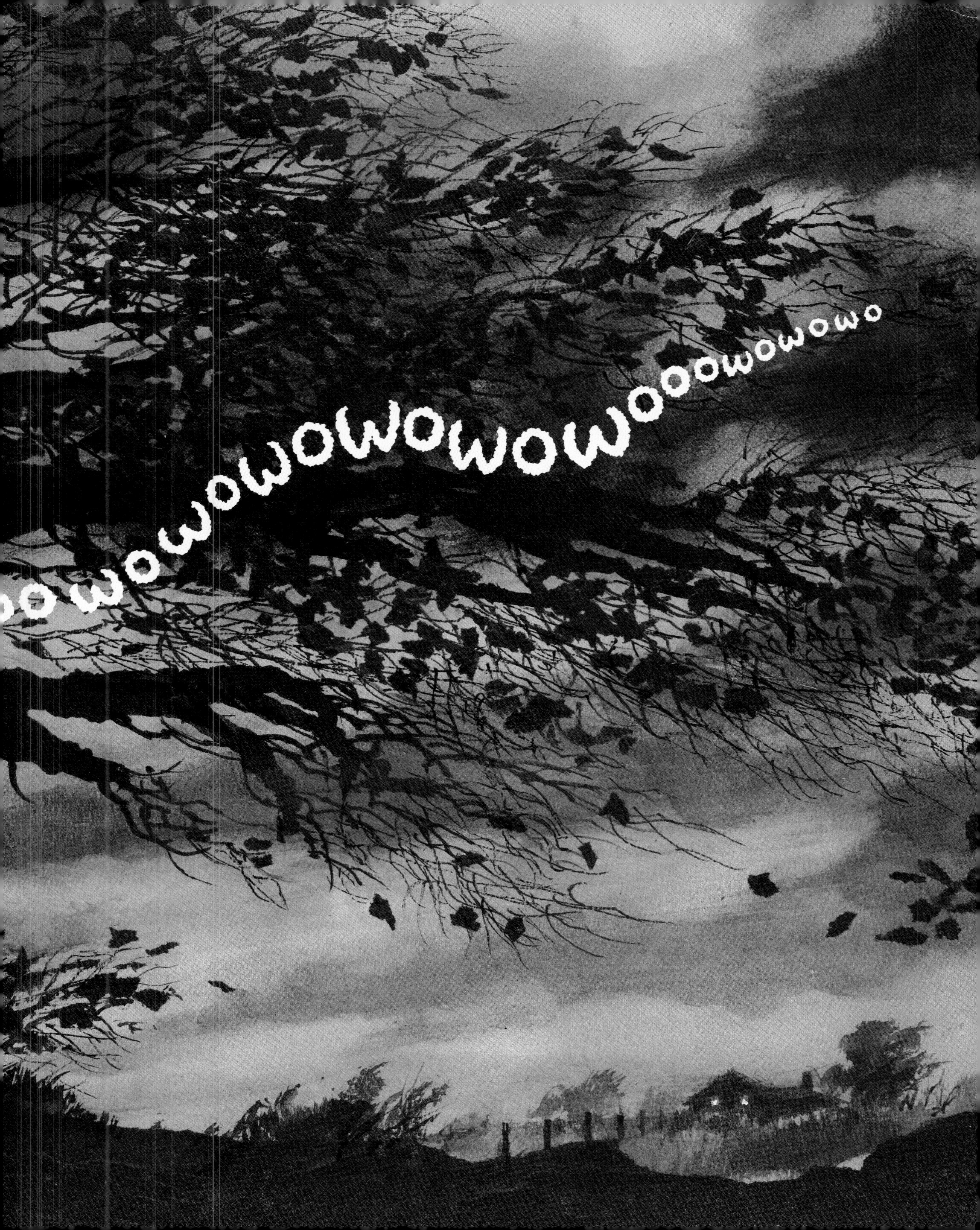
oowowowowowoWOWOWOWooowowowowo

Oh! Oooooohhhh!

We ran . . .
my sister and I . . .
Oh how we ran!
We ran . . .
all the way home . . .
as fast as we could. . . .
We set the bucket down . . .
flopped on the ground . . .
gasping . . .
for breath. . . .

"Oooo,"
  my sister said.
"I was so scared. . . ."

"Me, too,"
  I said.
"I saw the ghost. . . .
  Did you?"

"Yes,"
  my sister said.
"Don't tell Mama. . . .
  She'll worry. . . ."

"But she'll know,"
  I said.
"We spilt a lot of milk."

"That doesn't matter,"
  my sister said.
"I'll put some water in the bucket.
  She'll never know the difference.
  . . . Say! Where's your hat?"

"Oooo . . . my hat. . . .
  I lost it. . . ."
  I said.
"I lost it!"

"Where?"
  my sister said.

"Back there . . ."
  I said,
"b-b-by the Ghost-Eye tree. . . ."

"Oooo,"
  my sister said.

"But it don't matter,"
  I said.

"Yes it *does* matter,"
  my sister said.

"No,"
  I said,
"it makes me look stupid."

"It does not!"
  my sister said.
"It's a beautiful hat.
  Come on. . . .
  Let's . . .
  Let's go get it."

"No."
  I said,
"it don't matter.
  Really, it don't matter!"

Up she jumped,
that sister of mine,
and took to the road
that led through the town,
to the halfway tree,
the Ghost-Eye tree,
where my hat lay fallen
on the haunted ground.

"Ellie! Ellie! Come back!"
I cried.
"Ghost-Eye'll get you!
He's right by your side!"

But faster than foolies
that flash through your mind,
Ellie came back
leaving Ghost-Eye behind.

"Here's your dumb hat,"
  my sister said.
"It makes you look stupid."

"It does not,"
  I said.
"It's a beautiful hat."

I put it on my head,
pulled it down
over one eye . . .
to look tough . . .
like Mike Barber. . . .
I'm tough!
I said to myself.
Real tough!
I ain't 'fraid
of no ghost.

But . . .
since that dread night
at the halfway tree
when Ghost-Eye tried
to frighten me,
by some lucky chance
I'm never around . . .
when Mama wants milk . . .
from the end of the town. . . .

SQUARE FISH
An Imprint of Macmillan

THE GHOST-EYE TREE. Text copyright © 1985 by Bill Martin Jr and John Archambault.
Illustrations copyright © 1985 by Ted Rand. All rights reserved.
Printed in China by RR Donnelley Asia Printing Solutions Ltd., Dongguan City, Guangdong Province.
For information, address Square Fish, 175 Fifth Avenue, New York, NY 10010.

Square Fish and the Square Fish logo are trademarks of Macmillan and
are used by Henry Holt and Company under license from Macmillan.

Library of Congress Cataloging-in-Publication Data
Martin, Bill.
The ghost-eye tree / by Bill Martin Jr and John Archambault ; illustrated by Ted Rand.
Summary: Walking down a dark lonely road on an errand one night, a brother and sister
argue over who is afraid of the dread Ghost-Eye tree.
ISBN 978-0-8050-0947-7
1. Children's stories, American. [1. Ghosts—Fiction. 2. Fear—Fiction. 3. Brothers
and sisters—Fiction.] I. Archambault, John. II. Rand, Ted, ill. III. Title.
PZ7.M356773Gh 1985   [E]   85-8422

Originally published in the United States by Henry Holt and Company
First Square Fish Edition: September 2012
Book designed by Victoria Hartman
Square Fish logo designed by Filomena Tuosto
mackids.com

35 34 33 32

AR: 2.3 / LEXILE: NP